Everybody Loves Bernie

A book of bedtime stories from a legendary Grandpa

Stories by Bernard Gross

Published by Rachel Kerschhofer
Illustrations by Alexandra Hall-Pinner

Table of Contents

Dedication

This book contains real bedtime stories.

They are the tales that legendary Grandpa, Mr. Bernard Gross (aka: Bernie), used to tell his kids and grandkids. One day, Bernie's grandkids, named Rachel, Lauren, and Keith, decided to put their Grandpa's stories into a book. This was because they wanted to pass his fabulous stories down to future generations. That means kids, living now, and many years from now, that are dreamers, just like they were. Children with wild imaginations, huge hopes. It doesn't matter if they have a legendary Grandpa or not. Because in these pages, you'll find Bernie himself, bringing to life legends that only a brilliant, loving grandfather can think up. Making you laugh, cry, and feel like one of his own.

And that's why everybody loves Bernie!

Once upon a time,

there were two brothers, one named Ro, the
other named Ver. The two brothers were called
The Rover Boys.

They both **LOVED** milk.

"Now listen up kids.
Back in my day, milk used to be delivered in glass bottles to your doorstep, like a newspaper is delivered today, or like your mail is delivered by the mailman. So each house had a 'milkman'. You did not go to the grocery store to pick up milk. You had to wait for the milkman to deliver those glass bottles filled with milk, so you could drink it to help you grow big and strong. Now back to my story about the Rover Boys."

The Rover Boys

The Rover Boys loved milk SO much, that
every day, Ro and Ver would anxiously
wait for the milkman to arrive so that they
could drink the fresh bottles. The milkman
would come by their house super early
each morning, before anyone else in the
house was awake.

The Rover Boys knew the sound of the
milkman's truck, and before it was even
light outside, Ro would listen for that

Vroom, Vroom!

and pop out of his bed.

Ro would turn to his brother, aggressively tapping him on the shoulder, whispering,

"Ver! Ver! Wake up! The milkman is here!"

The Rover Boys would tip toe to their front door and wait with their ears pressed up against the door until they heard that Clink! and knew that the milk bottles had been placed on their doorstep.

The Rover Boys

Then, when they heard the milkman's truck drive to the next house, they would grab the bottles of milk in a rush and drink every last drop.

Ro went, *Gulp, gulp, gulp.* **"Aaaahhh!"**

while Ver went, **Glug, glug, glug.** *"Mmmmm!"*

Ro and Ver would tip toe back to their beds and sleep happily with their bellies full of milk, until they heard their mom gasp:

"Where has all our milk gone?! How are we going to have any milk for dinner or for cereal?"

Ro and Ver, awakened from their milk coma, rushed out of bed, acting startled.

Ro said, **"Maybe a squirrel drank the milk."** Ver agreed.

Their mom concluded, "Well, I guess we can make due this one time because the milkman will be back with more milk tomorrow morning. I'm sorry boys. I know how much you both love your milk."

Ro and Ver looked at each other and smirked.

The next morning, Ro and Ver woke up to the sound of the milkman's truck and listened for the Clink! Again, they drank up all the milk with a

Gulp, gulp, gulp. "Aaaahhh!"

and a, Glug, glug, glug. "Mmmm!"

and fell back asleep.

The Rover Boys were awakened by their mom screaming into the telephone at the milkman.

"Where is all our milk?! Every morning, we see empty milk bottles. What kind of milkman delivers empty milk bottles?!"

The milkman was stumped. He tried to
reassure Ro and Ver's mom: "I know I delivered
milk to your house this morning. And the
bottles were full of milk."

She did not believe him and said, "Just don't
let this happen again! I have two growing
boys that need their milk in order to grow big
and strong!"

The next morning, Ro listened for the milkman's truck

Vroom!

and quickly woke up Ver so that they could drink all of the milk. The milkman dropped the milk off at their doorstep

Clink!

and Ro and Ver heard him walk

Step step step

away from their door.

The Rover Boys proceeded to open the door and start drinking all of the milk as usual, when the milkman popped out from behind the bushes next to their house and yelled at the Rover Boys,

"Hey! Stop that!"

This time, the milkman had not gone back to his truck and driven down the street for his next delivery. He had waited to find out what was happening to his full bottles of milk and had caught the Rover Boys red-handed.

Before Ro and Ver could sneak back inside, the milkman grabbed them and rang the doorbell.

He told the Rover Boys' mom what Ro and Ver had been up to. She got really angry and gave them a long time out.

The Rover Boys

Ro and Ver's mom apologized to the milkman, and told him they would be happy to increase their milk order by 6 bottles so that everyone could be happy and have enough milk to drink.

The End

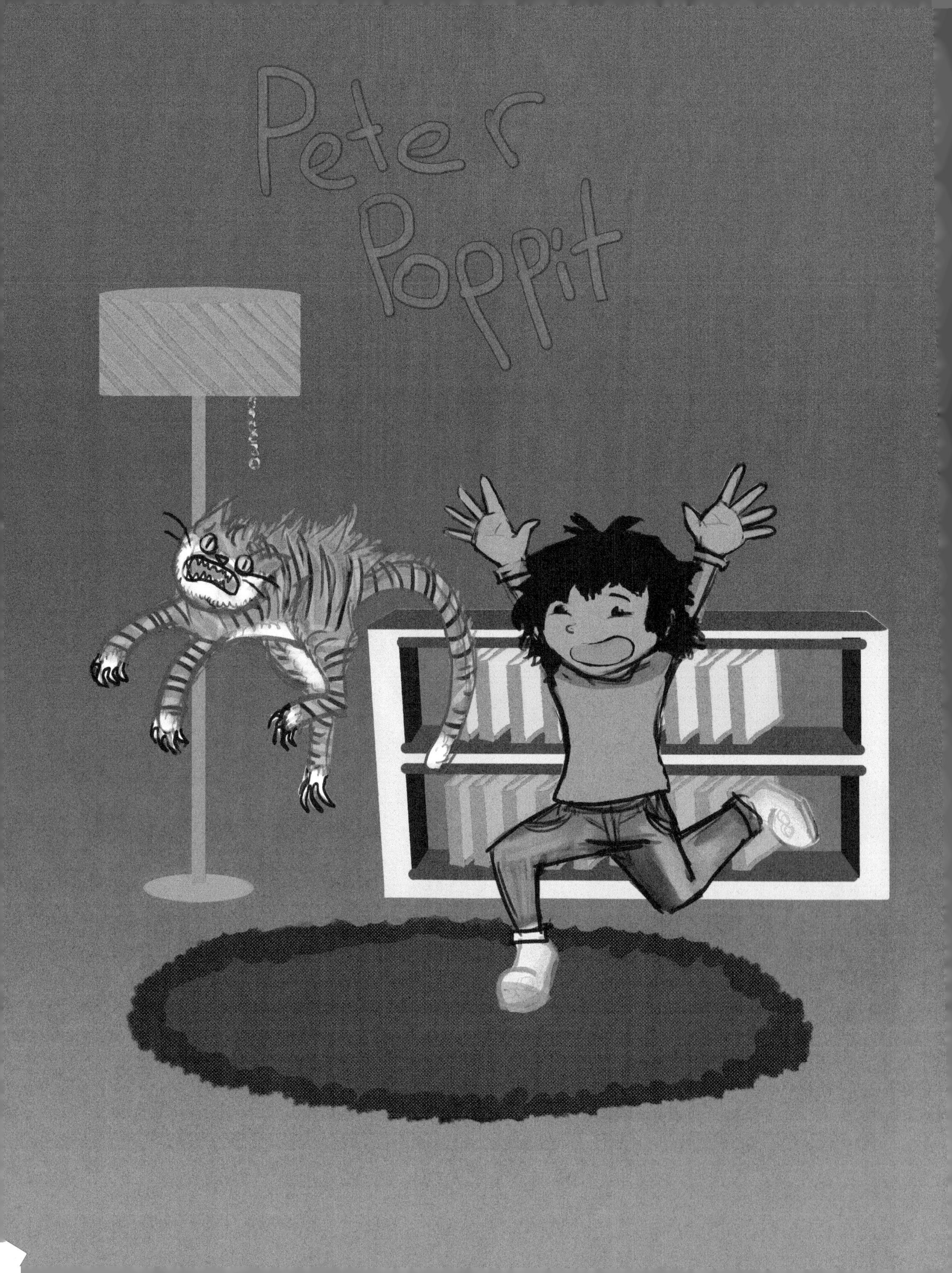
Peter
Poppit

Every night,

Peter Poppit's father would relax on his easy chair, quietly reading the newspaper. Peter Poppit loved to scare his father. He would tip toe, tip toe, ever so quietly, ever so quietly, tip toe,

"BOOOOOOOOOO!"

His father would be so caught off guard that sometimes the papers would fly all over the living room. He would get upset and yell,

"Peterrrrrrrrr!"

Well, when that got old, Peter decided to scare his grandma next. To scare his grandma, Peter followed the same routine.

He tip toed, tip toed, ever so quietly, ever so quietly...

"OH HELLO Peter! How are you?" his grandma said.

Well, this was a first. Peter had never been caught before. He was shocked.

"Grandma, how did you know I was coming?"

"Why, I could hear your shoes squeaking, Peter," his grandma said.

After that, Peter decided he would try to scare his grandma again. This time, he took his shoes off and wore only his socks.

Peter began to sneak up on his grandmother and

tip toe, tip toe, ever so quietly, ever so quietly...

"Ouchie!!!"

Peter exclaimed when his socks caused him to slip and fall onto his bottom on the hard tile floor. His grandma rushed to Peter's aid to help him back up.

After yet another unsuccessful attempt to scare his grandmother, Peter was determined to scare her this time. He took off both his shoes and socks and began to *tip toe, tip toe, ever so quietly, ever so quietly...*

"Aaahhchoo!" Peter sneezed.
"Bless you, Peter", Peter's grandma said.

Frustrated, Peter scurried back to his room to plot his next plan, but hard as he tried, nothing came.

Discouraged, Peter sulked his way back to the living room.

Through the open door, Peter saw his grandma in the kitchen, facing the counter, mixing batter for a cake.

Instantly, he knew this was his chance.

So barefoot, sockless, and all sneezed out, Peter proceeded to

tip toe, tip toe, ever so quietly, ever so quietly, tip toe,

"BOOOOOOOOOOOOOO!!!!!"

....

Peter Poppit

Peter Poppit

This time, Peter caused his grandma to throw the mixing bowl into the air so that the spoon and batter went all over the kitchen, even the floor and ceiling!

"*Now THAT was fun,*" Peter exclaimed with excitement.

Unlike his dad, Peter's grandma wasn't angry at all. In fact, she couldn't stop laughing,

"*Now THAT time you got me Peter.*"

Peter kindly helped his grandma clean up the mess and make more batter as they cracked up about how well he had gotten her.

Pretty soon, Peter was exhausted from sneaking around all day and found himself lounging in his grandma's living room, enjoying a piece of her delicious, homemade cake.

The End

There once was a boy named Dickeydickeyrumbanohsorum-
barbarbishkiishnomaynoellomenopennykokamishkoshucks!

"That's right kids. Repeat after me.

His name was:
Dickey-Dickey-Rumba. Oh-so-rumba.
Bar-bar-bishki. Ish-no-may-no.
El-lo-men-o-penny-ko-ka-mish-ko-shucks!

Good! Now back to my story."

Dickey Dickey Rumba

Dickeydickeyrumba loved to swim in the lake near his house with his friends. One day, Dickeydickeyrumba was in the lake swimming with his friend, Tom. They were having a great time.

Then, all of a sudden Dickey (that's what Tom called him for short) started shouting,

"Help me. Help me. I'm drowning! I'm drowning!"

Tom quickly swam over to save him only to find Dickey laughing. ***"Just kidding. I wasn't drowning. Gotcha!"*** Dickey said.

Tom rolled his eyes, swam away and said, "That was scary Dickey. You shouldn't play tricks like that. You better not do that to me again."

Well, guess what Dickey did the next week, and the week after that?

Finally, Tom said, "That's it Dickey. Next time you do this, I won't be here to swim to you." Dickey and Tom didn't talk for 2 weeks.

Then, 2 weeks after their fight, Dickey was swimming in the same lake. He was having a good time. All of a sudden, he started shouting,

"Help me! Help me! I'm drowning! I'm drowning!"

Only this time he wasn't joking; he was actually drowning!

Tom was walking across the bridge next to the lake and heard Dickey, but because Dickey had tricked Tom like this so many times before, Tom was not going to fall for it again.

Luckily for Dickey, there was another person around the lake that heard him and replied, "What's that? Who's that?"

And so Dickey told him:

"I'm Dickeydickeyrumbaohsorumbabarbarbishkiishnomaynoellomenopennykokamishkoshucks and I'm..."

but before he could say drowning, Dickey was already gone.

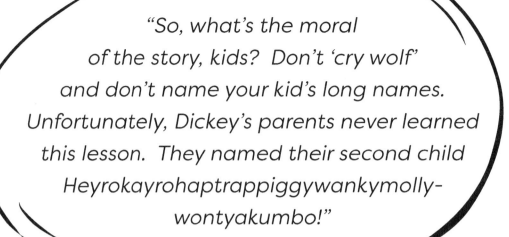

"So, what's the moral of the story, kids? Don't 'cry wolf' and don't name your kid's long names. Unfortunately, Dickey's parents never learned this lesson. They named their second child Heyrokayrohaptrappiggywankymolly-wontyakumbo!"

The End

Once there was a girl named Sarah.

All the other kids made fun of her because one of her legs was shorter than the other one, and to make things worse her name was actually Sarah Shorter.

Only her teacher Miss Jones stood up for Sarah. Miss Jones would tell the other kids,

"Now be nice to Sarah, class. She is pretty and smart and she is kind to all of you."

Sarah Shorter

But, cruel as kids can be, they continued to taunt Sarah and underestimate her strength.

It wasn't until years later that Sarah impressed her classmates. It was high school senior graduation and Sarah had received the highest grade in the whole high school, earning the honor of being class valedictorian. She had been accepted to Oxford University and was going to study biochemistry on a full scholarship.

Even on that day, after all those years of bullying, Sarah expressed only love and kindness.

Sarah Shorter

She told her classmates in her big speech at the graduation ceremony:

"Some would say I had it hard growing up. That I faced adversity. But, all of that is okay because, through it all, I had faith in myself. I even had faith in those that made fun of me because I believed one day they'd wake up and embrace those who are different. So, today, I'm happy for all of us, and how far we've come."

At the end of Sarah's speech, Jimmy Smitts, one of the worst bullies, found himself standing up to clap. At first, everyone was shocked, because he had been the meanest to Sarah.

But then he said,

"Great speech!"

and everyone in the room knew he meant it.

So with that, others stood and clapped for Sarah.
More bullies, more kids. Even the kids that had been
bullied worse than Sarah.

*Pretty soon, no one was
afraid and the crowd
was roaring with
cheer.*

In that moment,
Sarah's classmates
were finally able
to accept her even
though she had one leg
shorter than the other and
her name was Sarah Shorter.

After the graduation ceremony, they came up to her, wished her luck, and apologized for making fun of her all those years.

It was finally a new beginning.

Jimmy, along with the rest of the bullies, regretted making fun of Sarah and wished they had been her friend. She could have helped them to do better in school and get into great colleges like Sarah had done.

Sarah forgave all of the bullies, went on to win a Nobel Prize, and married Jimmy.

Jimmy started a nonprofit focused on raising awareness on bullying and helping victims of bullying.

Together, Jimmy and Sarah taught their kids never to make fun of someone because of how they look or how different they may be, since what truly matters is the kindness in someone's heart.

The End

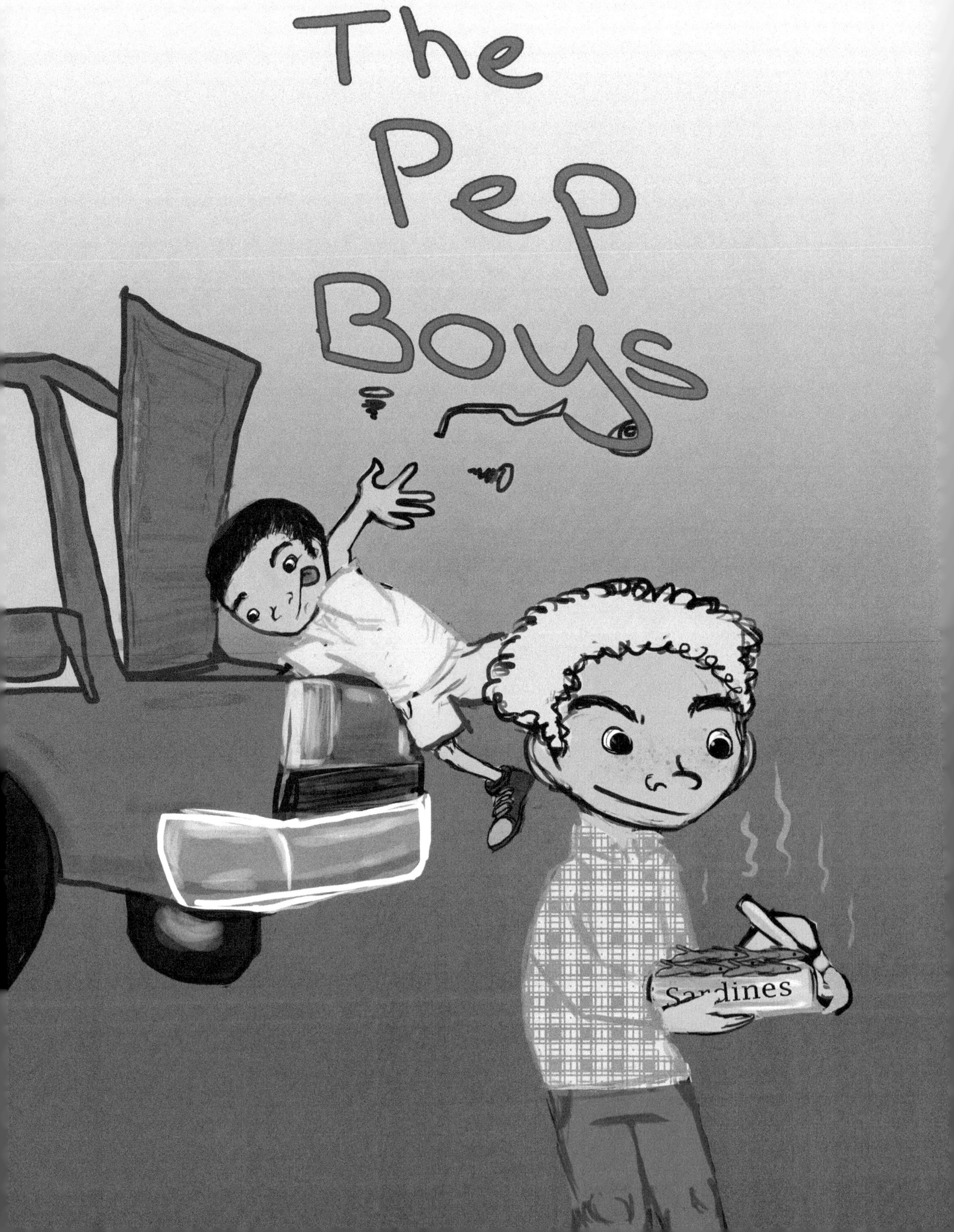
The Pep Boys
Sardines

Peter and Paul Pep were the sons of the owners of the famous **Pep Boys** auto shop chain.

In the early days, before Pep Boys became such a success, Peter and Paul were mischievous, young boys. They would always pull off pranks on customer's cars.

*They would **pop tires**, **put skunks in trunks;*** *they even did something to their science teacher's car and bribed him so he would give them an "A".*

But, can you believe it? All those years, all of those pranks, *they never got caught.*

Until one day, years later, it all came back to them.

It was when they were all grown up; Peter and Paul were both 21 years old. Their parents were now wealthy from the success of their auto shops, and had just bought them brand new cars.

On this important day, Peter went down to the rival shop, **Downer Girls,** to scope out the competition. The owner, Doug Downer, recognized Peter from when he was a little rascal, and knew that Peter and his brother had messed with his gas tank.

After all those years, he still held a grudge, so he took Peter's fancy new Rolls Royce and made it so that the steering wheel broke off 2 miles down the road. It got so bad that Peter veered off the road into a tree and his car was destroyed.

Well, this made Peter furious, so he called Downer Girls to complain. That's when Doug explained everything. How he had seen little Peter and Paul do their damage to his car when they were boys and how he needed to find justice.

Now, instead of deterring Peter, all this did was create an **all-out war** between the auto shops.

First, Peter married Dora Downer, Doug's first born daughter. Then, his brother **Paul married Denise Downer**, Doug's second daughter. And this was AFTER Doug had forbidden his daughters from interacting with the Pep Boys family!

So, Doug struck back.

He poached some of Pep Boys' biggest customers.

Then Peter and Paul struck back harder.

They threatened to move to Paris with their wives - did I mention these were Doug's only 2 children?

Well, finally Doug had had enough. He wanted to be a part of his daughter's and future grandkid's lives.

"After all, one day you will have grandchildren and come to realize that grandkids are one of the greatest joys, if not, the greatest joy of your lifetime, and you will not want to miss a single moment in their lives. Anyway, back to my story."

The Pep Boys

Doug Downer decided to end the feud. He brought both families together to bury the hatchet.

"Look," Doug said, addressing the Pep boys, *"you boys were a bunch of bored, little schmucks when you did that stuff to my car. I'm sure by now you have learned your lesson. But I am getting old. I can't take this battle any longer. So please, just stick around so I can be near my daughters. I beg you! I'll do whatever it takes!"*

The Pep Boys

That's when, always with expansion in mind, Peter and Paul made their proposition:

Pep Boys and Downer Girls merging their shops into 1 auto shop conglomerate, so both of their businesses could thrive.

Oh, and Peter and Paul admitted they were bad kids - little devils with nothing else to do besides mess with real cars as their toys.

In the end, both families embraced each other and laughed it off.

"Let's hope our little ones don't turn out that way," said Paul. Denise replied, "Oh, that reminds me, I'm pregnant."

And with that, both families were shocked, burst out with excitement, and vowed to raise the grandkids with just the right amount of discipline.

The End

CPSIA information can be obtained
at www.ICGtesting.com
Printed in the USA
LVOW06*2109251217
560754LV00002B/2/P